A FAMOUS
CHRISTMAS MEMORY
THE PUMPKIN BREAD RECIPE FIASCO

**THE PERFECT PUMPKIN
BREAD RECIPE INCLUDED**

This fun and heartfelt Christmas story starts with a touch of adventure and a bit of magic and leaves you with the perfect pumpkin bread recipe to create your own famous Christmas memories.

PROLOGUE

Upon the loss of her mother, the time of great sadness, Famous discovered her mother's journals with a letter telling Famous to follow her path to where she had found her. Famous began a journey of self-discovery. She traveled by train, boat, and plane meeting interesting characters all along her path. A path that led to her destiny of breaking curses and a magical family.

I dedicate this book to my amazing, supportive, and helpful husband. He was key to the completion of the book. Also, to my stunning daughter Kayla Dondrea who pushed me to write it, when I was giving up on writing and helped with the initial idea.

Famous and Destiny, the nearly identical twin cousins spent the day talking about their upcoming Christmas adventure to Ireland. The months had passed, winter was upon them, and Christmas would soon be here. They made plans to join the family in Ireland for a happy Christmas celebration.

Famous stared out the window of her grandfather's cabin, looking out as the snow began to fall again. The white sky seemed to be drifting slowly down dusting the treetops. The once bright green meadow filled with flowers had now become a sea of white.

Famous hadn't planned to be in the forest this long.

She had planned to be back at her cottage in New

York getting things ready before her trip back to

Ireland, but her and Destiny had been having such

a lovely time getting to know of each other's life

before they met and learned about The Monster In

The Forest. Now, she had fallen behind and was

concerned the trip was going to be much more

tasking than she had planned. Jeremiah, her

grandfather, had gone back to Ireland weeks before

leaving her and Destiny behind to join him and the

family for the holidays.

She imagined how much her life had changed, magic, curses, princesses, and a big family she had never known. She wished she had known them growing up but would never give up the childhood she had had with her mother.

Destiny strolled in the kitchen, seeing Famous in deep thought. "What are you thinking about?"

"A lot of things I guess, the trek out might be daunting, and I need to go to New York before I go to Ireland. I haven't been back in months and who knows how long I will be gone." Famous chuckled. "Are you still coming with me, or do you need to get back?"

Destiny gave her a sly smile, "No way am I going back until you do!"

Famous stood up, "Well then, we have to get ready, close Jeremiah's cabin for winter and get out of here. Winter is coming and we don't want to be stuck in it."

The day ran into the next preparing for the trip. They used a list from their grandfather to prepare the cabin for winter, which was more work than they had thought it would be. The snow continued to fall, and the concern continued to grow. The outside world might as well have been a million miles away with no internet or phone possibility, it could be a challenge to get a train when they get to the station. Famous thought about their map and the possibility of using it as a means of travel. Jeremiah had warned of the unnecessary use of magic on several occasions. Was this one of those occasions?

She could hear him say, "We only use magic, when there is no alternative." Glancing out the window at the snow falling and the depths rising she wondered if this was such an occasion.

"Probably not!" Famous said aloud as she got up from the table.

Destiny glanced back at her, "probably not, what?"

"Oh, I was just wondering, if this was an occasion to, you know, use a little magic, to help us on our way."

Destiny seemed to be considering it before agreeing that it was probably not considered a need type situation, but she also didn't seem opposed to it either. "You know the snow is getting pretty deep and who knows if we can even get a train. It might be worth thinking about."

Famous sat in the living room on the bean bag next to the fire considering the idea.

"We are running later than we had planned." Famous said, like she was considering a quick jump into the map wouldn't be a terrible idea. She also considered they hadn't had a lot of experience with it either. Only the one time from Iceland to the forest. Remembering back to the curse and their fathers stuck in the forest.

Destiny broke her thoughts, "And I am sure you need to do some things before we can head back to Ireland, we don't want to be late getting back."

"But we probably shouldn't use the map and amulets, right?" Famous added

Destiny shrugged, "I suppose, but..."

Famous interrupted, "Buuuuuuut I still need to find my mom's pumpkin bread recipe, get winter clothes, and check on stuff." Her words were drawn out like she had a million things to do. Famous glanced over at her backpack, thinking her map was right there. In her heart she knew that her family would never approve.

Famous glanced around the cabin, the furniture carefully covered, the windows all closed and boarded up, taking all the remaining food to the cellar, padlocks on all outer doors and every other detail Jeremiah had put on the list to winterize the cabin, all items were carefully done. She checked and double checked the list. "List is complete, Destiny." Famous announced.

She packed the book of Wisdom, her map, journals, put the amulets in her pocket.

"We still need to find a safe place for this book, I guess we should have sent it with Jeremiah, but he was sure Dublin was no longer a safe place."

They had considered all the options and talked in great detail about the trip. It was decided that they would see how the trek went and only use magic if absolutely necessary.

With snowshoes, parkas, and backpacks they began their trek to the train station at first light. It had been a long time since Famous had been to the train station. She had made her first and only trek from there in the dark of night many months ago. Since then, she had traveled to several countries, freed a princess, broken curses, and even been kidnapped. She had found where she came from, her heritage, and her family. Now with only a hand drawn map from their grandfather, they set out to find the station.

Destiny and Famous dredged along the snow-covered paths for hours chatting. "Famous, what was Christmas like when you were growing up?" Destiny questioned.

"It was wonderful, my mom and I would bake for nearly the whole town. We would have such a lovely time delivering fresh baked goods to the shelters, churches, and just anyone really. Some retailers would even order our baked goods. Mom would save the money we earned for a girl's outing or a special occasion just for us."

"What did you bake?"

"Pies, cakes, breads, oh there was this one year, there was a bumper crop of pumpkins, what a year that was." Famous laughed and she thought back to the time. "Mom decided we would make pumpkin bread, but she couldn't find the family recipe. We had so many pumpkins on the porch. All the ladies in the town had donated pumpkins from their patch." Famous drifted off laughing, "So you see we had pumpkins everywhere.

We frantically searched for the recipe, Christmas was only two weeks away and we had promised pumpkin bread for the Christmas bake sale, several retailers, shelters, and the list goes on, more than fifty loaves had been promised."

They stopped to take a breath and a drink of water. Destiny watched as Famous became animated about the lost recipe she was laughing so hard she leaned against a tree. Snow dropped from the tree lifting the weight from the lower branches. They watched as they bounced upwards. Destiny laughed at Famous's snow-covered head.

They quietly continued for a little while. "So, what happened with all the pumpkins? Didn't anyone else have the recipe?"

"Umm, no, not this recipe." She continued to ramble on with her story, "Sorry I forgot where I was after the whole snow nonsense. Hmmm, oh yeah, so mom was frantically looking through boxes, The books in the bookcase, she had dug through every drawer. I mean we had a small place, how could something so important be lost?

I was preparing the pumpkin, which means digging out the flesh and mashing. Most people just buy canned pumpkin. This year we had been so busy that we hadn't even decorated for Christmas yet." Famous was giggling again as she demonstrated a pile of pumpkins on the porch and in the living room

as she played out the memory.

"What did you do?"

Famous was still giggling at the thought as she

suddenly fell into a hole. She grabbed Destiny's arm

and took her with her. They fell for what seemed

like forever landing firmly with a thud into a pit of

darkness.

"What happened? Famous? Are you okay?" Destiny felt the ground around her. She looked up and could only see a speck of light above, thinking to herself that it seems impossible that they fell down such a small hole. She continued to feel the ground around her and call for Famous. A slight movement startled her as she heard a groan from Famous. "Are you okay?" She repeated

"I think so," Famous began checking for pain in her limbs. Everything seemed fine, well except the fact that the hole above looked a mile away, "How are we going to get out of here?"

Destiny shrugged, "Isn't funny that things like this happen to us so often, we don't even panic anymore?"

"Yeah, hilarious!" Famous felt the ground for her backpack. "I think I have a flashlight in here somewhere." She says as she begins taking out the contents. "Maybe we can use the map. It's so dark, hmmm, visualization?" She chatters on absent mindedly. She noticed Destiny was being too quiet. "Destiny?"

"Hmm?"

"Are you okay?"

"I'm not sure, my leg hurts pretty bad." Destiny tried to move it and winced in pain.

Famous snatched out her flashlight and shuffled over to Destiny. She began examining her asking if this or that hurt every time, she touched a different spot. Destiny yelped when she got to her ankle.

"Let me see, I need to find something to wrap that, then I think it's time to use the amulets and the map. I only hope we don't do more harm to that ankle; remember how we landed last time." Famous began looking for anything she could use to wrap Destiny's ankle. She removed her scarf and wrapped her ankle tight. "I hope it's not broken, maybe we stay here tonight to see if it feels better in the morning. What do you think?"

Destiny sat up and drug her legs to lean against the wall, dirt and snow cascaded down. Concern showed on Famous's face from the glow of the flashlight. "Let's rest a bit and then we will figure out what our options are. Tell me more about the pumpkin bread recipe fiasco."

Famous sat next to her and held her hand. "Okay, let me see where was I? Oh yeah, I was crushing pumpkin and my mom was frantically looking for the pumpkin bread recipe. Well, I had drug all the pumpkins in the kitchen, dining room and living room, our house looked like a pumpkin patch."

Destiny giggled, "I bet that was a sight!"

Famous laughed, "It sure was. Mom was digging out

all the boxes of Christmas decorations. She thought

perhaps it had gotten put in there. We were trying

to remember when we had made it last. Which of

course brought up a bunch of fun memories but

wasn't at all helpful. Then I thought, let's just make

pies instead, but mom was like, no we promised

bread and they shall get bread."

Famous grabbed her pack and handed Destiny some cinnamon bread. "After nearly tearing the whole house apart, we didn't find the recipe."

"What did you do?"

Famous sighed, "We baked, we tasted, we laughed, then we tried again. We knew the ingredients, at least we thought we did. So, it was a matter of finding the right combination. So, we baked, we tasted, we got into a flour fight, we laughed, and did it all again." Both girls were laughing.

"Did you ever get it right?"

"I can't tell you that yet, it will ruin the story. After baking for two whole days, we had kept every combination we had tried written down so we wouldn't try them again. My mom decided we needed to take a break. She said that since she had dragged out the decorations, she declared we were going to go get a Christmas tree. We went to a lot near our house a friend of ours had for a charity. There were no trees left. We tried where another lot had been, but it was closed, so no luck there.

Mom was in such a state, but she would not let this break her spirits. She was driving through town talking about the pumpkin bread recipe. She said, It looks like we will have to find an alternative to find a tree. Maybe find one of those cut it down yourself places. Driving further through part of the

town they rarely traveled through she noticed a tiny

decorated Christmas tree in the window of a small

curio shop. It was the Store of Mysteries; I was

never allowed in there! I guess we know why,"

Famous chuckled.

STORE OF
MYSTRIES

Destiny rolled her eyes, "I think your story is getting off topic."

"Do you want to hear it or not?"

Destiny laughed, "Okay, okay, I am invested, keep going."

Famous handed Destiny the water and began her story again. "My mother actually parked and told me to stay put. She marched right into that shop. I would love to know what she said because out she came with that tree of lights."

"She did not!"

"Yes, she did, I swear! So anyway, we went home and put the tree in the tiny living room of our cottage. Wait 'til you see my little cottage, I miss it, but it will never be the same without her."

Destiny put her arm around Famous and hugged her close. Time had ticked by, and darkness fell on the forest. Snow had covered the hole above and tiny flake fell into a pile in the center of the ground. Destiny had fallen asleep, Famous was at work reading books full of magic she had brought. Several of them are everchanging, so there was a good chance she could find something that applied to their situation.

Famous shivered as she laid her parka on Destiny. Thinking there must be something she could do to warm the pit and keep Destiny warm. Her pocket suddenly felt warmth radiating from it. The amulets, she dug into her pocket and pulled them out. They were shining as bright as the sun, Famous notice a small tunnel she had been unable to see before in the darkness.

She crawled to the entrance and shined her flashlight in. Too dark, she crawled a little further, raised and opened her hand, but the amulets had dimmed. Famous focused all of her energy on the amulets until they glowed once again. The tunnel was long and dark. She was nervous to leave Destiny alone. She inched her way as far as she could go and still see the outline of Destiny's feet. The tunnel continued far beyond her sight.

Famous suddenly felt a surge of fear, thinking what might live in a tunnel such as this and began backing out. A shuffling noise behind her made her nearly jump out of her skin. Destiny had awoken and was at her heals. "You almost scared me to death, Destiny!" She screeched.

Destiny snorted trying not to laugh, "Imagine how I felt, I woke up and you were gone. At least I thought you were until I saw the dim light coming from this tunnel."

"Well back up, would you? Who knows what kind of creatures live down there."

Destiny and Famous crawled backwards to the pit from which they came. Famous could see Destiny was favoring her ankle, but it didn't appear to be as bad as she feared. "How's the ankle?"

"I'll live, not going skiing any time soon, but I can sure crawl." They both laughed. "As long as I don't drag my foot and keep it pointed upwards, I think I can move, should we see if there is an exit to that tunnel? It might be our best chance."

Famous considered it for a second, "But it also might be a dead end, or worse." They both sat back with a sigh. "I used the amulets for light in the tunnel." She held out her hand to show Destiny. "I know it's not safe to use magic because it always leaves a trace or something, but what choice did I have."

Destiny patted Famous's hand, "It's fine, were fine, so we're in a hole in the forest, no worries for us, right?" Her smile beamed and calmed Famous at the same time. "We have been doing great for months. I hardly think that will cause a ripple in time, haha. So, what do you think, if it helps, I think we should go for it. I also think you should finish your story; I am dying to find out how that ends."

"Really? That is why you fell asleep at the good part." Famous chuckled as she crawled forward, the tunnel was dark, she could feel the soft dirt and smooth rocks beneath her hands. Destiny followed her into the darkness. Famous clicked on her flashlight, the dim beam barely lit the path in front of her. The tunnel was surprisingly well dug, her thoughts wandered to question how the tunnel was dug out. Destiny's strong Irish accent seemed louder in the tunnel. "Now that I think of it, I don't remember ever having pumpkin bread in my whole life."

"What, no way, wasn't there some when we were at your, I mean our grandmas."

"Well, if there was, I didn't have any. Anyway, go on with your story." Destiny said as they inched forward in the darkness.

"Ok, here we are with a pumpkin patch, boxes, a tree, all piled in this tiny living room. The kitchen had loads of papers scattered on the counter with different variations of pumpkin bread." Famous's voice trailed off for a second

Destiny was hanging on her every word and trying not to think about the pain emanating from her ankle with each stride forward. She didn't want to alert Famous to her anxiety. Suddenly she ran directly into the back end of Famous. "What's up?"

"Shhh, I thought I heard something," She whispered. Famous held still and cocked her head to listen. Small scratching noises possibly or was it her imagination. A voice in her head said to turn back. Another voice said to move forward. Which voice to listen to is always a question in her mind.

"I don't hear anything," Destiny whispered back. "This may be our only way out; I don't see how we can scale the dirt walls of the pit." Destiny was pushing her forward.

Famous went forward a little further, "We don't even know if we are heading out or deeper into the earth, we could end up in some crazed animal den." She reached into her pocket and pulled out the amulets. Her heart was pumping so hard the warmth had grown uncomfortable. The light radiated to a blinding glow, Famous strained her eyes to see ahead.

A vision of her mom appeared in her mind, a soft voice saying it's okay Famous. She crawled forward a little further and came to a dead end. "Well, I guess this is the end of the road." She announced as dirt fell from the top of the tunnel and a rumble above startled them. "What do you suppose that was, Destiny?" More scuffling and dirt falling. "I think it's going to cave in on us, move back. Hurry, move back!" She tried to go back, but Destiny didn't budge.

The heat from the amulets felt like fire in Famous's hand. A pulsing vibration caused a wave of energy like an electrical surge. Dirt continued to fall, Famous was certain it was an earthquake until a dim light from the moon and the cold moisture of snow touched her face. The frosty cold air took her breath away. Famous and Destiny began digging, clawing at the earth to escape the darkness of the tunnel.

Several minutes that seemed like hours passed, the light from above grew larger as they dug and crawled towards the sky. Finally, they crawled out of the wet ground and sat on a heap of snow. "We made it!" Famous exclaimed as she let out an exasperated breath.

"Yeah, now what?" Destiny waved her hand as if to say they were lost. Both taking in the snow-covered forest, looking for some sign of recognition. Destiny opened her pack and dug out her map. Each girl had been given a map that helped them find their way, with the magic amulets and the right incantation they could use the map to travel to a certain location. "I say we jump for it."

Famous shook her head, "We have only done that once, I don't know if we can pull it off again. How can we be sure we will end up in the right place?"

"Well, I can't exactly walk, and you can't carry me, so what choice do we have? Besides how am I ever going to hear the end of this pumpkin bread story if I freeze to death in the forest. Destiny held her map and watched it as it unfolded. She watched as the line appeared and then faded to their next destination. A dot appeared on the map in New York. "See, it's just a dot the line faded, so we jump and that is where we will land."

Famous opened her backpack and pulled out the case with her map in it. She slowly pulled out the small rectangle, held it in her hand and watched as it opened. "Yeah, I have only the dot, I guess I had made the decision before I opened it." She looked closely at the map recognizing the landing spot, "That looks like home, I'm hoping for the yard. It would be terrible to land on the roof." She let out a nervous laugh.

They put on their backpacks and sandwiched the amulets between their hands, heat radiated as before. Destiny wobbled as she stood on one leg. "Ok, Destiny, just like before, repeat after me." They closed their eyes and began the chant. "On our map there is a dot, take us now to that very spot. On our map there is a dot, take us now to that very spot." The earth rumbled, Destiny was losing her footing, Famous held her hand as tight as she could.

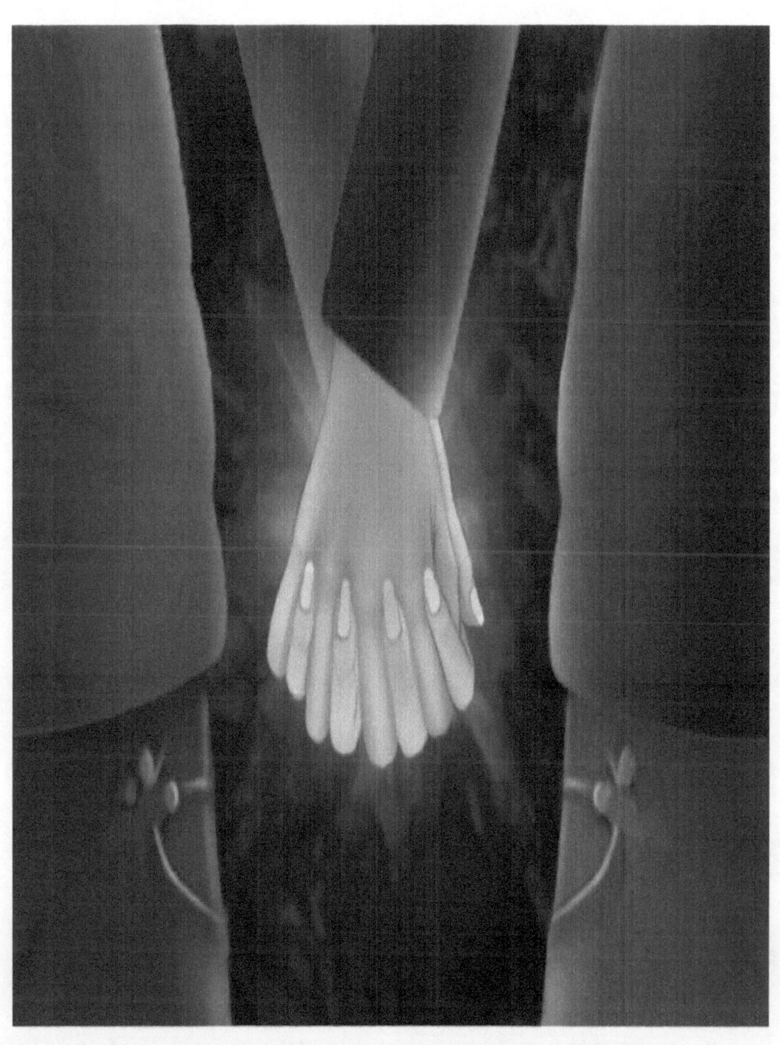

A crack of lightening made them nearly jump out of their skin Famous screamed as the world began to swirl by. Her nails dug into Destiny's hand. A bright glow, brighter than they had remembered emanated from the amulets in their sandwiched between their hands.

Famous continued chanting and Destiny joined in. "On our map there is a dot, take us now to that very spot." The earth appeared to open and swallow them. They were falling and falling, "Don't let me go Famous."

Famous squeezed her hand even tighter, "I've got you." Destiny screamed in pain as they hit the ground. They laid there for several minutes staring up at the sky. Snow was falling, Famous could see a shadow of a tree in her peripheral vision. "Are we still in the forest?" She asked as she started to sit up.

Destiny didn't answer right away, she was still lying flat on her back with her eyes tightly closed. Slowly she opened them and began to sit up. "I am going to say no!"

Famous quickly sat up, "We're here, we made it!" They were in the yard of the small cottage Famous had grown up in. She could see the back door had been over ran by ivy growth, and the lawn needed a good mowing.

A light from the apartment above the garage indicated her renter may be home.

She helped Destiny to her feet and hobble to the back door. Famous pulled a small rock from the outer wall where she had hidden a key. The door creaked as she pushed it open.

It was just as she had left it, the kitchen she had many memories with her mother. "This is it Destiny, can you imagine this room full of pumpkins?" Famous clicked on the light to illuminate the small kitchen, she visualized her mom standing there with Flour on her face laughing.

 Famous clicked on lights as she carried on with her story. "So anyway, we were here, right in this spot." Famous walked into the living area, when my mom screamed, I've got it! Oh, my goodness Famous, my mom said laughing and laughing. Honestly, I thought she had gone mad.

Famous pointed to the small stairway to her loft bedroom telling Destiny that is her room and then to her mother's room at the base of the staircase.

Destiny hopped about grabbing walls to steady herself. "You can't stop there, what happened? What did your mom scream about?"

"The recipe silly, she thought she remembered where it was." Famous paused for dramatic effect.

"Well, did she remember? Did she find it?" Destiny asked excitedly.

"My mom dropped the tree and ran out the door saying she knew where it was. I was just standing there wondering where she was going. I followed her out to the garage. I thought there was no way it could be out there. We kept our car and tools only in the garage. But there in the corner was a box of every recipe my mom had ever made."

"Wait, what? Why?"

Famous giggled, "Crazy story, the year before and many years before that, the whole town loved all of my mom's cooking and baked goods. She got this this idea in her head to make a recipe book, she got all of her recipes together and put them in this box. She was pretty free spirited, it was no surprise it didn't go past that idea in her head. She literally put it out of her mind, it was a busy year, months had gone by. It completely slipped her mind." Famous laughed, "Can you imagine?"

Destiny stood there staring at Famous, "Really? That was you great Christmas story?"

Famous gave Destiny an annoyed look. "Hold on, we took the box in the house and read through each and every recipe. There was no pumpkin bread recipe to be found."

Famous took a long look around, dust covered nearly everything. She walked in the kitchen, opened the fridge, empty, then the freezer. It was still half full.

"Famous, you have got to finish this story. Where was the recipe? Did you find it? What made this Christmas such a special memory?"

She walked into her mom's room; her favorite perfume smell had faded but was still vaguely present. "My mom, that's mostly what made it so special." Famous turned back to Destiny, "Okay, the recipe was in the box, but you seemed disappointed by my story." Famous walked back to the living area, Destiny hopped behind her. We spent the next ten days baking pumpkin bread together."

They paused at the wall filled with photos of Famous and her mom, Famous pointed at one area with them handing out bread at a shelter. Then a nursing facility. Another of them standing in the kitchen covered in flour with dozens of loaves of pumpkin bread on the counter in front of them. One last photo of them sitting in front of a pile of pumpkins.

"We should do that!" Destiny announced

"Do what?"

"Bake pumpkin bread for the shelter, nursing facilities, I don't know, the hospitals. We will do it for your mom."

Famous's eyes got misty, "What about Ireland, we leave in a week?"

"I guess we better get busy!" Destiny said with determination.

"I'm thinking we'll have to order a pizza for tonight there is nothing in that fridge." Famous dug her phone out and plugged it in. She watched as it slowly came to life. A million thoughts came to mind, letting neighbors know she was back, so the police wouldn't be called was top on her list. She sent out a few quick texts and called the pizza place.

Famous buzzed around the cottage, turning on lights and the heat. She grabbed ace bandages and blankets from the closet. Slowly she unwrapped Destiny's ankle and removed her boot, "I don't think it's broke, can you wiggle your toes?" Destiny wiggled them and nodded. Famous moved her foot one way and then the other. Destiny winced a few times as she moved it up and down. "Maybe you should stay off it for a few days."

Destiny shook her head, "There is no time for that, you better find that recipe and start making a list."

"Hmm, I wonder, where that recipe is now?"

"You have got to be kidding?" Destiny said as a knock at the door made them both jump. Famous peeked out the window before opening the door, she signed the slip, said thank you, and grabbed the pizza. Her and Destiny devoured the whole pizza while Famous rattled off more stories about the town and the library where she used to work.

Destiny had fallen off to sleep on the couch. Famous covered her up and climbed the stairs to her bedroom. She had always loved the loft bedroom. She could see nearly the whole downstairs from her bed. She struggled to fall asleep, visions of baking with Destiny filled her head. Those visions were soon replaced by dreams of memories of her and her mother.

The morning came quickly, Famous could see Destiny was still asleep. She tiptoed down the stairs and into the kitchen. She started a much-needed pot of coffee and walked over to the bookcase. On the shelf was a large cookbook, only it wasn't a book at all, it was a box that looked like a book.

Famous had found it at a flea market shortly after the pumpkin bread recipe fiasco. She bought it for her mother for her favorite recipes. She pulled the book box from the shelf and sat at the small table where her and her mother had sat together many times before. She wiped away the dust and smiled at the memory of her mom when she opened the wrapping paper, they must have laughed for a solid five minutes. Famous opened the box and just as she remembered the top recipe was the pumpkin bread recipe as her mom said it always needed to be on top to remind them of their famous Christmas memory and the pumpkin bread recipe fiasco.

She wrote her list and calculated how much of each ingredient she would need. Then took a quick inventory of what was left in the pantry. She left a quick note for Destiny before heading off to the store.

Destiny awoke to the smell of coffee and carefully calculated how she was going to get the cup back to the living room after hopping into the kitchen. It was a task but she moved the coffee from one spot to the next until she accomplished her goal, thinking how lucky she was that it was a cozy little place. She saw that Famous had left the open box of recipes next to the note with an arrow and a smiley face. Destiny admired how the box looked like a recipe book.

She sat on the couch sipping her coffee and thought of her family. She saw Famous had left her phone and wondered if she could make international calls, she tried but it didn't go through. She logged into her email and sent off an email to her mom and grandma.

Hello Mum and Mawmaw,

Famous and I are safe, it's a long story, but were at her place in New York. We are going to try to make the plane, but something has come up. I think it's really important for Famous. We're going to bake pumpkin bread for some of the shelters and care facilities like she did with her mom. So, we may have to change our flight. I'll let you know as soon as I can.

Love you forever,

Destiny

 Miles and miles away in Ireland, Angelica, Famous and Destiny's grandmother and Darla, Destiny's mother were having a late afternoon tea in the garden when the email came through on Darla's phone. She read it aloud to Angelica, "We could bop over and give them a hand." Darla said, nonchalantly.

With a big grin, Angelica said, "I suppose it wouldn't hurt, maybe ring up Ellie, you know how much she was a big part of bringing Famous back to us after the princess curse was lifted."

Darla agreed, "I'm sure Famous would love that."

She immediately called Ellie and she was overjoyed

at the idea. "Ellie's in and with a little magic, we can be there by noon to surprise the girls.

Famous had to grab a cab to bring her home from the grocery store. She had bags and bags of flour, sugar, spices, eggs, oil and canned pumpkin. There was no time to find that many pumpkins and bake and puree them. She had also stopped at a thrift store and was lucky to find Destiny crutches. finally stopped by a pharmacy and bought an ankle brace. The cab driver was kind enough to help Famous unload, so she gave him a nice tip before sending him on his way with a wish for a Merry Christmas.

Destiny was elated and relieved to have the crutches and ankle brace. It was quite a job to put the groceries away.

Famous was quick to fix them a sandwich before the

girls went to work on the first batch, Famous placed

the recipe on the counter.

It was written in her mother's handwriting. She

smiled as she traced the words.

Pumpkin Bread

Preheat oven to 350 degrees grease and flour four

bread pans or decorative tins.

3 cups sugar

3 $\frac{1}{2}$ cups flour

2 tsp baking soda

2 cups pumpkin puree or 1 15-16 oz. can of pumpkin

2 tsp each nutmeg, ground cloves, cinnamon

1 tsp vanilla

1 cup water

1 cup oil

4 eggs

Mix all dry ingredients well, add wet ingredients continue mixing until all are added, and mixture is smooth. Bake for 40-60 minutes depending on pan and oven. It is done when toothpick is inserted and comes out clean.

Famous began handing Destiny spoons, whisks, bowls, measuring cups and spoons. She was preheating the oven when there was a knock on the door. Famous looked at Destiny, she shrugged, "Are we expecting someone?"

Famous shook her head, "Not that I know of." She peeked out the window and let out an excited scream, "I can't believe it!" She yanked open the door and there stood Angelica, Darla, and Ellie.

"How…" Famous stuttered.

"We've come to help." Angelica gave Famous a quick hug and breezed past her to the kitchen where Destiny stood leaning on her crutches. "Oh my, what has happened to you child?" Destiny and Famous took turns telling of their story and the story about the pumpkin bread recipe fiasco, the short version as Destiny called it.

"It took me days to get the whole story." Destiny exclaimed.

"I can't believe you are here!" Famous squeezed Ellie so hard she could barely breath.

"Me either, I wouldn't miss the chance to bake with you like before and like I did with your mom. What a great Christmas memory this will be." The women chattered as they mixed the ingredients. Every hour a new batch went into the oven. They laughed and took several pictures to add to their walls of pictures.

Famous called the places she had volunteered at with her mom to make arrangements for them to bring bread over the following several days. It was a long day of baking, laughing, and the kitchen was wrecked with flour. Famous watched for a moment and tears of joy streaked her cheeks, Destiny put her arm around her. She whispered, "Thank you." The ladies all gathered around her for a group hug.

Ten hours of baking, forty loaves of bread were placed all over the house on cooling racks and wax paper. The house smelled heavenly as the evening came to an end.

Darla and Angelica shared Famous's mom's room.

Famous smiled as life returned to the room being

filled with the love of family and the smell of

pumpkin bread. Destiny had the couch as crutches

and stairs don't mix. Ellie bunked with Famous.

The days following were filled new special Christmas

memories of love and giving.

The End

Happy Christmas to all my Irish friends and adopted family.

Merry Christmas to my American friends and family

Alexis Anicque, wife, mother of two grown children, and nana to four grandchildren. Self-proclaimed traveler and adventure seeker. Enjoys spending her time writing, telling stories, jumping on planes, trains, or buses looking for her next destination. Lives in a cottage in the woods but loves city life and public transportation

Read other Famous Adventures
by Alexis Anicque

Finding Famous

Famous embarks on a journey, where she learns the fairy tales her mother had told her were stories of her adventure to Finding Famous. A magic journal to an epic adventure.

296 pages

Famous Destiny; The Monster In The Forest

The adventure continues, Famous has broke the curse on the princess, now can she solve the mystery of the monster in the forest?

266 pages

Coming soon

Which Witch is Which Famous

Looks are Deceiving

Read more books

<u>alexisanicque.com</u>

www.ingramcontent.com/pod-product-compliance
Lightning Source LLC
Chambersburg PA
CBHW031549310726
48971CB00008B/2684